CASTING
LILY

CASTING LILY

Holly Bennett

ORCA BOOK PUBLISHERS

Library and Archives Canada Cataloguing in Publication

Bennett, Holly, 1957-, author
Casting Lily / Holly Bennett.
(Orca limelights)

Issued in print and electronic formats.
ISBN 978-1-4598-1450-9 (softcover).—ISBN 978-1-4598-1451-6 (PDF).—
ISBN 978-1-4598-1452-3 (EPUB)

I. Title. II. Series: Orca limelights
PS8603.E5595C37 2018   jC813'.6   C2017-904542-3
C2017-904543-1

First published in the United States, 2018
Library of Congress Control Number: 2017949699

Summary: In this high-interest novel for teen readers, Ava lands a
part in a professional outdoor theater production.

*Orca Book Publishers is dedicated to preserving the environment and has printed
this book on Forest Stewardship Council® certified paper.*

Orca Book Publishers gratefully acknowledges the support for
its publishing programs provided by the following agencies:
the Government of Canada through the Canada Book Fund and the
Canada Council for the Arts, and the Province of British Columbia
through the BC Arts Council and the Book Publishing Tax Credit.

Edited by Tanya Trafford
Cover design by Rachel Page
Cover photography by iStock.com/brown54486

ORCA BOOK PUBLISHERS
www.orcabook.com

Printed and bound in Canada.

21 20 19 18 • 4 3 2 1

To all the players, young and old, who bring stories to life before our very eyes.

One

*F*inally the bell rings. Lunchtime. I make a dash for the door, determined to get ahead of the crush and stake out a corner seat in the noisy little lunchroom. By the time Char shows up, I have the page loaded up on my phone and have made it halfway through a bag of chips.

"Char, check this out!" I thrust the phone under her nose.

"Hi, Ava. Hang on," she says. She sets down her lunch bag and pulls out its contents one by one. Then she arranges the various containers to her liking and settles into her chair. Slooooowly.

"*Charlotte.* Just look, will ya?"

She takes my phone, peers at the screen, pretends to adjust her glasses. "Your phone screen is so small—what am I looking at?"

I fake-smack her, but halfheartedly. I'm too excited. "It's a casting call for that summer theater. Mill Pond Farm? They're doing a play about kids. They want *kids* to audition!"

I've been taking drama classes and acting in school plays since I was little, but this is a chance to spend the summer with an actual professional theater company. Ever since I stumbled across the ad, I haven't been able to think of anything else.

"That's cool," says Charlotte coolly, handing back my phone. "Are you going to audition?"

I stare at her. "No, I showed you because I'm not interested. *YES*, I'm going to audition! *Of course.* But Char, you should too."

"Haha." She's only giving me half her attention. "I'm your friend who doesn't act, remember?"

"No, look." I scroll down and start reading aloud. "*Mill Pond Farm depends on our volunteers! Would you enjoy helping with production, front of house or concession sales? If so, please attend the volunteer-information session following either audition time.*" I pin her with my eyes.

"The costumes you made for *Bye Bye Birdie* last year were brilliant! And admit it—you enjoyed it, even if I did have to talk you into it."

Char looks thoughtful. "Yeah, that might be cool. But it's the whole summer."

"Yeah, but it's the summer on a beautiful farm. It'll be a blast. And"—I lean in, because this is the real reason I want her to sign up, the thing that might persuade my parents to let me do it—"if we're both going, we can stay at each other's places when our families are away."

She chews her food, saying nothing. I wait, trying not to look desperate. Finally she looks up at me.

"I'll think about it."

Typical Char. But it's good enough for step two.

* * *

I need a calmer, more Charlotte-like pitch for my parents. I want them to see this as a reasonable, logical thing to do, not some crazy teen impulse. Especially my father, the insurance accountant. *PleasepleasepleaseDaddy?* doesn't work with him, as I've learned the hard way.

Think, Ava.

It's a great opportunity...That sounds mature and logical, right?

Almost like a summer job...Yeah, he'll like the sound of that. No need to add *only without the money.*

Keeping my skills up for school...Hmm, maybe not that one. That might lead to talk of my math and science marks from last term.

I resist the urge to blurt it all out during dinner. I stick to my plan, which is to catch them at 8:40, twenty minutes before their favorite TV show comes on. For some reason, they never record it for later—they watch it on regular TV, every Tuesday night, with a bowl of popcorn. It's like a lame date, I guess. Anyway, my cunning plan is to talk to them when there is just barely enough time available. They will be half distracted as we near the nine o'clock mark.

It works, kind of. They have a ton of questions I can't answer. Is there any transportation provided? What kind of supervision do they have for kids and teens on-site? How late would I get home every night?

I do, at least, have an answer for one: "What about our camping trip?"

"I would have to miss it. But I can stay with Charlotte," I assure them. "And she's going to volunteer for the theater, so maybe she can stay with us when her mom goes away?"

"Let's go back to *our* trip," says my mom. "Summer goes by fast, and, as you say, this will be like a job. It's a real commitment—you can't just walk away mid-August if you decide you want a bit of vacation after all."

"I know that!" I'm irritated now and not hiding it very well. "I know what's involved in putting on a play. This will be better for me than a camping trip." Understatement. I loved our summer campouts when I was little, but spending two weeks crammed into a tent with my parents and little brother, playing endless rounds of rummy, has seriously lost its appeal.

In the end we make a deal. I will audition, and if I'm offered a part, I can only accept it on the condition that all my parents' questions are answered to their satisfaction.

I escape to my room and do a little happy dance on the bed. Then I text Charlotte.

They said YESSSSS!!!

I lie awake for a long time, thinking about the audition. What should I wear? What will they ask me to do? What should I prepare? I try not to think about how awful I'll feel if I don't get in.

Two

The auditions are at the downtown library. I arrive a bit early, but there are already a few kids, some with their parents, sitting in the library "lounge." Some lounge—it's basically a big bare room. I stake out a spot against the wall.

A few minutes later a boy settles in beside me. He's blond and slim and looks a little older than I am. He slips off his coat and hat and then fishes in his backpack and pulls out a big envelope. He glances over at me.

"Trying for a lead?"

I nod. "But I'll take anything."

"Hmm." He frowns slightly, just enough to make me feel I've said something wrong. There's an awkward silence while we pretend to watch the little kids running around.

"I got a new headshot for this," Blond Boy announces out of the blue. "I thought my old one was too babyish. What do you think?" He reaches into his envelope and pulls out some papers and an eight-by-ten glossy, which he hands to me. I have to admit, it's pretty impressive. He looks both older and better-looking than in real life.

"Nice." I hand it back. "I don't have a head-shot," I admit. Was I supposed to? The ad didn't say anything about photos.

"No? It's pretty standard." He gives me a once-over. "Don't you have a résumé either?"

I shake my head. I'm feeling nervous now, wondering if I'm in over my head. All I have with me is a scribbled list of plays I've been in, in case I forget if they ask me. "Can I see yours?" I say.

"Sure." He passes it over, and I scan the page. Kiefer Monroe. He's done quite a lot of acting, mostly school and kid-oriented plays, same as me, but a couple look more serious. And then I see he has listed a play that came out two years before I was born.

A New World Voyage: Babe in arms

Babe in arms? He put down an acting credit from when he was a baby? Wow. I'm not feeling so intimidated anymore. In fact, I have to work hard not to burst out laughing.

"You've had a lot of experience," I say, proud of my serious tone. Call it acting practice.

A young woman with a clipboard appears, and parents quickly round up the younger kids. She hands out a form for each of us to fill out. I pull out my list and get started.

"I brought a résumé," Kiefer says, holding out his envelope.

"That's great, but we'd still like you to fill out the form," she says. "It helps if everyone's information is in the same format."

Soon the younger kids are ushered in ones and twos to the audition room. I finish the form. I wait.

"Ava...Oljark?" The woman shrugs and scans her eyes across the room. She has spectacularly long cornrows that swish across her lower back as she turns.

I *so* need a stage name. "Olejarczyk," I say, for about the thousandth time in my life, and follow her down the hall. In the audition room, three people sit in a row of chairs, facing an open space with a single chair at the front. I am instantly nervous.

Every audition I've ever done has been held in some school or church gym, in front of everyone. I guess that should be *more* nerve-racking, but somehow it isn't, not for me. Here, in this quiet room with only me and the…I want to say *judges*, it feels like a lot more pressure.

The woman who escorted me in takes a seat beside the rest of them and introduces herself as Amanda, the assistant director. Then she names everyone else. Stephen, the director, is a skinny guy with no hair on top, but a full dark beard. The last two are Terry, the stage manager, and Mel, the music director. I sit in the empty chair and will myself not to fidget while they look over my info sheet.

Finally the director looks up. "You have a lot of acting experience for a"—he glances down—"fourteen-year-old."

Is it conceited to nod? I decide to just smile. "I love acting," I say, then cringe. Stupid, obvious thing to say. But the director nods politely.

"What's your favorite role so far?" he asks.

I'm torn, so I decide to name two. "Playing the princess in *The Paper Bag Princess* was the most fun," I say, "but I was proudest of playing Rosie Alvarez in *Bye Bye Birdie*."

"Why's that?"

"It was the first musical I'd been in where I had to sing solo, and I don't really consider myself a singer." Too late I see that this, too, is a dumb thing to say—why offer my weakness on a plate to them? There's nothing to be done but plow on. "So it was a bit scary, and I had to work hard both on my singing and my confidence."

They seem to like that answer, and after a few more questions they give me an outline of the play—it's about poor kids from England who were sent to Canada in the 1800s to help farm families. Then they invite me to perform my monologue. Everyone interested in a lead or supporting role was asked to come prepared to perform a solo scene. It had been *so* hard to decide what to do. Charlotte thought I was crazy to try Shakespeare, but Ms. Lovell, my drama teacher, encouraged me to aim high. And I *had* gotten good laughs from it when we did our "Scenes from the Bard" unit.

I take a deep breath and stand up, and as I push my chair back out of the way, I get an idea.

I tip it over onto the floor, so it can stand in for a body. My scene is from *The Tempest*, where Trinculo discovers Caliban lying on the beach. "*A man or a fish? Dead or alive? A fish: he smells like a fish; a very ancient and fish-like smell...*"

When I'm done, they thank me and Amanda says, "You have a very clear voice," which sounds to me a bit like, *I have to find* something *nice to say, and that's all I can come up with.* But she smiles like she's given me a great compliment. Just as I'm about to exit, tail between my legs, the music director finally pipes up.

"Just one more thing. Would you sing 'Happy Birthday' for us, please?"

I can't have heard that right. "Pardon?"

"'Happy Birthday.' You know, the song. Could you sing it for us."

"Um, sure. Sorry, I didn't realize this was a musical. I could have prepared something."

They chuckle a bit and wave their hands reassuringly.

"No, no, it's not a musical," Amanda explains. "But there will still be some singing, mostly in groups. We just want to know who can carry a tune."

I feel like an idiot, but I sing for them anyway, thank them and then do my best not to bolt out of the room.

I have a strong urge to run to the washroom and cry. But I don't. I march back through the "lounge," pretending all is well. I even smile and wave at a girl I remember from last year's Christmas pantomime. Then I text my mom that I'm ready to go home.

I already know I won't sleep tonight. Instead I will replay every dumb thing I said and did in the audition and just pray that, despite it all, they will call me.

Three

got a callback to read for the part of Lily! When Amanda phoned with the news, I wanted to shriek with excitement. Instead I forced myself to be serious and write down all the instructions. Then Amanda asked to speak with one of my parents.

I think they feel a lot better about my doing this now. Amanda said she'd send home an information sheet after my second audition. If I'm chosen, there will be a meeting with the parents before rehearsals start to answer any last questions.

I have a scene to learn before I go. It's a bit funny and also sad. From what I understand, Lily and her sisters have been sent to one children's home, and her brothers to another. They don't get to see each other at all. In this scene, Lily's brother Walter has somehow gotten some girls' clothes and put them on so he can sneak over to talk to Lily. He's being sent to Canada, and he wants her to come too. But she has her little sisters to look out for and doesn't want to leave them behind. They're trying to work it all out in a big, whispered hurry, knowing Walter could get caught any minute.

So I guess they will be auditioning for Walter at the same time as for Lily.

It's hard to tell what kind of person Lily is from just one scene. I know she's only eleven years old. And I don't think she's scared to go to Canada with Walter. It's more that she thinks she should protect her sisters. So she's not being sucky. Or maybe she just feels she's in an okay place, so why take a risk? Either way, Walter is the one who's impulsive and angry, so Lily has to be more steady. I feel a twinge of disappoint-ment—it would be more fun to play someone spunky and rebellious—but whatever. I set myself to work. Amanda said I didn't have to fully memorize my lines, but I intend to.

* * *

"Really. They called you back?"

It's Blond Boy, and while he doesn't exactly stress the *you*, his tone is pretty insulting all the same. So great, I'm auditioning with a full-of-himself dude who has already decided I'm not good enough. I feel a flare of anger, but I remember the lecture Ms. Lovell gave us: *In real life, you can like a person or not—I don't care. But when you're onstage, the only thing you feel for that person is what your character feels.* I swallow my anger and offer a smile I hope looks real.

Stephen, the director, brings us in together. I notice Amanda sitting at the back of the room and say hi. She smiles but stays where she is—observing, I guess. They've set up some props at the front of the room. A table and chairs and, to mark the doorway, one of those poles with hooks on it for hanging up coats. "Oh, and this," Stephen says gleefully, pulling out an old-fashioned bonnet with a flourish and plopping it on Kiefer's head. I see Kiefer's mouth tighten, and suddenly I feel much more relaxed.

"So we'll do a quick run-through," says Stephen, "just to get familiar with the scene. I'll play the house mother. Ava, you are sitting at the table. Questions? Then let's dive in and see how it goes."

I bend my head and start pretending to sew. Kiefer stands in the doorway, waving and coughing to try to get my attention. My start of surprise feels really fake, and our hug is even worse, but once we get to the dialogue, things smooth out a bit. Kiefer is good, and the way he plays Walter, angry and kind of rough, with just one desperate idea in his head, makes it easier to find Lily's response. She cares for him, but he's not really making sense. I can see how she's torn, tempted to just run off with him and take the chance. After just one very rough run-through, I can already tell that Kiefer would make a good Walter. But it doesn't make me like him any better.

We come to the end, with me promising, "I'll find you wherever you go!" Then we just stand there awkwardly, waiting for Stephen to say something. He's nodding, scratching his beard, and my self-confidence crashes. *Maybe Kiefer was good, but I was so bad he can't even think what to say.* Then he smiles.

"Okay, that was a great start. I can see you've both already thought about your characters and what they're like. So let's talk about the scene itself, and then we'll work on the blocking a bit." He sits on the table and asks, "Do you have any questions about your characters, or about what they are saying here?"

Kiefer shakes his head and looks smug, like, *I've got it all figured out.*

I do have some questions, and even though I'm a bit afraid of sounding stupid, I decide to speak up.

"When Lily promises to write, and to find Walter, does she really think she'll be able to? I mean, he has already lost track of his brothers, and he doesn't know where in Canada he's going. So...does she not realize how hard it will be to keep in touch, or is she just saying that to reassure him and to persuade him to go? Or have I got it wrong?"

"You don't have it wrong, and that's a great question," Stephen says, and my mood pops back up. "What's your best guess, just based on what you've already learned about Lily?"

Ugh. I hate when grown-ups throw a question back at you like that. But I take a stab. "Well...a bit of both? She's only eleven, and maybe she can't face that they are all going to get cut off from each other. But her main goal right now is to keep Walter from getting in trouble, and I think she'll say whatever it takes to keep him from getting caught."

Stephen nods again. "That's very perceptive." Kiefer looks sour, and I admit I find that very satisfying. *Ha—take that, with your fancy head shot and résumé.* But then Stephen adds, "So how does that insight affect how you deliver those lines?"

Awkward silence while I try, and fail, to think of a reply. "I'm not sure," I admit.

"And that," says Stephen, grinning, "is why we have directors! Okay, let's work on a few things."

He brings some humor into the beginning of the scene by pacing back and forth (as the house mother) and having Kiefer alternate between trying to get my attention and dodging out of sight every time the house mother turns to face the doorway. "And we'll want you to be very awkward in your girls' clothes," he says to Kiefer, "but that will come much more easily once you're actually wearing them."

Geez, it sounds like Kiefer has the part nailed down already.

"Same thing when Lily excuses herself and you two duck out of sight to talk," he says to me. "You're trying to focus on each other and talk, but Lily, you're also keeping an eye out for the house mother or other staff and trying to keep Walter quiet."

When we get to the end of the scene, Stephen turns to me. "Try thinking of this. You have to push Walter away, but you don't want to let him go. You're afraid your promises can't be filled, but you want fiercely to believe they will be, so you say them with all the conviction you can muster. You know you might be saying goodbye for good, but everything is so rushed, and he's about to get caught. Think of all that, and then just say it how you feel it."

Wow. All of a sudden this dumb little scene seems to have so much more going on. We work through it from the start again, and this time when we get to the end, those words don't sound stupid—they sound brave and sad, and the little choky tremor that comes into my voice isn't even faked.

"Well done, both of you," Stephen says. "We have some other people to see, and we'll be in touch within the week." Amanda comes over and hands us our parent-information sheets, and we're out the door.

Two kids, a guy and a girl, are sitting in the waiting room as we leave. You can't have it, I think as I pass the girl. *I'm* Lily.

Four

June 30. I'm sitting in the back seat of the car with Charlotte, heading to Mill Pond Farm for our first day of rehearsals. There's a shuttle that goes to the farm every day, but Mom insisted on driving us today. I guess she wants to check out the place, make sure everything's okay.

Char is chattering away, wondering if she'll get to do much actual sewing and what the workspace will be like, but I'm too excited to listen very well.

It has been three long months since I got the call telling me I'd won the part. Then a package was delivered to the door—a letter, revealing that as a main character I'd be paid a "small honorarium" of $300, and a full script of *Doctor Barnardo's Children*, along with instructions.

I had to learn my lines by the first day of rehearsal. Which I have, but that doesn't mean I feel prepared. The next couple of months are one big question mark, and I admit I'm pretty nervous.

We pull into the "parking lot"—really just a big mowed field—and follow the signs to the barnyard.

"Oh my," says my mom. "I'd forgotten how lovely it is here." I turn a slow circle, taking in the whole space. The barn itself is L-shaped, closing off two sides of the space. They've built on a long second-floor balcony, with stairs down to the ground, and a sort of raised deck tucked into the corner of the L that can be used as a bandstand or set element. Across the barnyard, facing the long side of the barn, are the raised bleachers where the audience will sit. The fourth side is open, looking onto a little pond with a footbridge, rolling fields and hills, and neighboring farms. The sky seems so much bigger here than it does in the city.

Amanda comes over to meet us. She shakes hands with Mom and tells me there's a cast meeting at nine thirty. Then she turns to Char. "Charlotte, Beth is the costume manager, and she is really looking forward to meeting you. Come with me and I'll introduce you." Just then the shuttle bus pulls up, and about a dozen people, mostly adults, pile out.

"Hey, Ava!" I track the waving hand down to a familiar face and suddenly feel happier and more settled. It's Will. We met in drama camp last summer, and he was really fun to hang out with. If Will is here, I'll have a least one buddy in the cast.

I turn to my mom, who is still hanging around. "Mom, you can go home. I'm fine here. Look—it's my friend Will." Will grins hello to my mom.

"Well…all right. You have your phone?"

"Mom! Yes, don't worry!" By the time she turns the car down the laneway, I've discovered that Will has the other "young lead" role, playing Walter's friend Billy.

"Do you know who's playing Walter?" Will asks.

I'm about to tell him I'm not sure when a shiny SUV pulls up the lane. Somehow I'm not surprised to see Kiefer emerge. Oh well, win some, lose some.

* * *

The cast meeting is not exactly what I expected.

Everyone is introduced, of course. There's one other girl about my age, Kendra, who is playing Emily, "Old Walter's" granddaughter.

Stephen tells us more about the children known as "home children." Some were sent to the homes that Dr. Barnardo started. Others went to live with families in Canada. Some of them were treated well, but a lot of them had very hard lives. Then he says, "People shared their parents' or grandparents' life experiences—in some cases, very difficult experiences—with us, and their stories are actually in the script." He wants us to always treat their stories honestly and with sensitivity. "Remember," he says, "this is real history. And relatives of the people it happened to could be in the audience."

No pressure, eh? I want to joke, but it's clear this is no joking matter for him.

Then Amanda gets up, and she's all business. She hands out a rehearsal schedule and other papers and goes over a bunch of ground rules. It's all pretty confusing, and then we're told to take a break and reconvene at the "backstage lounge" at eleven.

I'm wondering how to pass the time when Will grabs my arm. "C'mon, let's explore!" He's practically bouncing out of his red Converses, grinning from ear to ear. "Man, this is going to be a great summer!"

I can't help but laugh. "Could you show a little enthusiasm?"

*　*　*

The backstage lounge is a bunch of old couches and armchairs arranged in a rough square in one corner of the barn. It also has a little kitchen area, which Amanda says we can use to prepare the lunches we'll have to bring for ourselves every day. When Will and I get there, Kiefer and Kendra have already claimed the two newest-looking chairs.

Amanda spends a long, boring time going over our schedules. Then she says, "Okay, enough of that. *WARM-UP!*" I jump at her sudden shout.

She gets us up and makes us run on the spot and do jumping jacks. She shouts out different animal names and makes us do animal calls (Kiefer looks really unhappy at this point). Then she moves us into a circle and pulls out a ball. We play this memory game where you recite a list of items and then throw the ball to someone else, who has to come up with a new item and then recite it all. It's corny, but it works. By the end of it we're all laughing and way more relaxed.

Kiefer, though. I know we have to be a team, and I'm trying. But there is something about him that just rubs me the wrong way. He thinks he's better than us—I'm convinced of it—and that scorn keeps oozing out of him.

* * *

Lunch is a chance to relax and hang out together. All the kids sit on the grass—the four of us, plus Charlotte and some other teen volunteers—and we're getting along great until Kiefer turns to Will and says, "It's weird, eh, that they cast you for this role? You must have been surprised."

"Why? Will's a great actor." I shouldn't butt in, but I can't help it. I guess I'm kind of mouthy that way.

"Yeah, but..." Kiefer eyes Will again. "You don't exactly look like you're from Jolly Old England."

My hackles rise. As I learned in drama camp last year, Will's mom is Ojibwe. Kiefer is obviously making a reference to Will's darker coloring.

"But y*ou* do." Will's voice is calm, even amused. I sit back, realizing he's more than able to take on Kiefer's nonsense. "You're going to look like a lobster by opening night, after a month of rehearsing in the sun."

Kiefer scowls but says nothing. *Good.*

* * *

I thought we would do the first read-through sitting around a table, but instead Stephen has us do it out in the barnyard. "For those of you new to outdoor theater," he says, "it's best to get a taste of it right from the start. That way you understand why we push volume so much during rehearsal. But don't worry—Mel will work with you if you're having trouble projecting your voice."

I'm already nervous, reading with all these adult actors, and it feels like the air is swallowing up my voice. Will, on the other hand, has a huge voice. It seems to carry for miles, even when he's talking normally. "My grade-two teacher was always telling me to use my 'indoor voice,'" he jokes. "She didn't seem to believe me when I told her I was!"

But I do know my lines, and as we work our way through the script I start to feel more confident. I get a better a sense of the other actors and characters. Gary, playing Dr. Barnardo, seems really nice. He's funny and takes the time to make us feel part of things.

Will has to check his script a few times, but it's clear he's a great choice for the cheerful, optimistic Billy, who is always joking around and looking on the bright side.

Kiefer tries to show off with an English accent. To my delight (I know—I'm a bad person!), Stephen immediately asks him not to. He is kind about it though. "It's a good idea, but there are too many issues with region and class, and it's too difficult to get a whole cast consistently doing decent accents."

After the read-through, Stephen gives us some general notes about the different characters. I'm getting bored and starting to zone out when he turns to me.

"Lily. I think the early Lily will come along quite easily to you, Ava—you've already made a great start on your own. Lily is dutiful but spirited, trying bravely to hold the family together, but too young for the job. We have to keep that idea that she's really just a child, no matter what she says." I nod.

"The big challenge in this role," says Stephen, "is later on, in the scene with her foster family and Dr. Barnardo. The audience has to really feel her suffering, and how she's been silenced by the reverend and Mrs. Talmadge. She is silently *begging* Dr. Barnardo to notice and rescue her, because apart from him she is completely alone. But when she realizes he won't be helping her..." He nods. "Yes. It's a key scene."

He moves on to Young Walter and Old Walter, and discusses how they can make the bridge from the boy Kiefer plays to the rough-edged, cranky old man played by his adult counterpart. I'm not listening though. I'm thinking about Lily's *key scene* and feeling a bit overwhelmed. The truth is, I don't get why Lily is so timid. But that's what rehearsal's for...I hope.

Five

It's amazing how fast we settle into a routine. We do warm-ups, we work scenes with Stephen or Amanda, we have lunch, we work some more. There's also a lot of waiting. On our downtime we hang out backstage or go on little hikes around the property or spread a blanket out in the field and relax. Poor Kendra is in completely different scenes from the rest of us, so she spends a lot of her time off on her own. I have a fair bit of time alone too—I'm trying not to be disappointed that the "kid" part of the play is mostly about Walter and Billy, and not so much about Lily. Sometimes I watch the other actors work. I figure I can learn a lot, and understand the play better, from watching the more experienced actors in action, but honestly a lot of the time it's pretty boring. I make a mental note to start bringing a book with me or, better yet, see if I can lay claim to the family iPad.

On Thursday I'm sent to see Beth about my costume.

When I arrive, Charlotte greets me with, "Welcome to my domain." The farmhouse living room and dining room have been converted into a sewing/fitting room and a giant closet holding all the costumes from past plays.

"*Our* domain," Beth corrects from behind her. Charlotte flushes, but I can see from Beth's grin that she is joking.

"You better watch out. Char's pushy that way," I warn. "Always trying to take over."

"She will one day," says Beth cheerfully. The word *jolly* jumps into my head. I've never met anyone who looks as jolly as Beth. "This girl has talent—I can already tell." She raises her hands to frame an imaginary sign. "Charlotte Lee, costumer to the stars."

Char looks even more embarrassed, but pleased.

Beth asks for my sizes, top, pants and shoes, and then gets out a tape measure. She starts calling out numbers to Charlotte, who writes them down on a sheet. There's a running commentary too, punctuated with Beth's cackling laughter. It bubbles out of her as easily as breath, it seems.

"Where's the rest of you?" she jokes as she measures my waist. Cascades of laughter. "Of course, you're still growing." She put her hands on her ample hips. "Still, I don't believe I was ever that slim, even as a child. But what the heck?" More laughter. "I'm a whole lotta woman, that's what!"

Beth is larger than life and loves color. She sports a long, flowing purple top over capri-length red leggings. Long loops of mauve beads hang around her neck and clatter as she works. On her feet are bright-pink Crocs. I kid you not.

Beth is as opposite to Charlotte as it's possible to get, and it's clear to me that Charlotte—quiet, neat, efficient Charlotte—adores her.

"Right, off you go." Beth shoos me out the door. "Charlotte and I will cook up something for Miss Lily to wear and call you back for a fitting when we're ready."

* * *

It's Tuesday of week two, and I'm staying with Charlotte and her mom. My family has gone camping.

It's fun being at Char's apartment, but whenever I'm at the farm, a knot of panic keeps growing inside me. I keep trying to push it down, but it pushes back up. Kiefer and Will are doing so well, and I...well, for one thing, I'm having trouble with my voice.

I must not be hiding it as well as I thought, because after our vocal warm-up Mel asks me to hang back.

"You seem frustrated, Ava. Is something wrong?" Mel is intense, and when she trains her eyes on me, there is no evading them. I squirm a bit. Sigh. Mumble.

"It's just...I feel like I'm yelling. To be loud enough, I have to yell. And that's not going to work in my last two scenes."

She shakes her head. "You're doing fine. Remember, we're training muscles here—your vocal muscles. It takes time. By opening night, you'll be ready."

"But Will—"

She cuts me off. "You cannot compare your-self to Will. Or to the professional actors, for that matter. Will is a special case—hardly anyone is born with a set of pipes like that. Everyone else has to go through what you are doing now. Trust me."

I'm not convinced, and Mel knows it.

"I tell you what. Let it go for a week. Do your warm-ups, remember what we've talked about—full breaths, loose throat, sending your voice beyond the back of the bleachers—but stop worrying about it. We'll get together on Monday or Tuesday, and if you aren't feeling more confi-dent by then, I'll schedule some private coaching sessions." She elbows me gently in the ribs. "But you won't need them."

"Okay." Forgetting about it seems like dumb advice to me. But her promise of help if I need it does make me feel better. "Thanks."

I run off to the mini stage where we often do the early work on scenes. Today will be the first try at Lily's visit from Dr. Barnardo. My stomach is full of butterflies. This, I realize, is what I'm *really* worried about.

Six

It's crazy how much trouble I'm having with a scene where I hardly even have any lines. The whole thing goes by so fast, yet somehow I'm supposed to burst into tears partway through.

So here's the gist. Lily is now thirteen or fourteen. Dr. Barnardo is visiting Canada, and he comes to check on Lily. She's been placed with a reverend and his wife in some tiny village out in the country. The reverend seems nice enough, but it's pretty obvious that the wife is mean, complaining about how much Lily eats and not wanting to let her take music lessons. Then Dr. Barnardo asks to speak to Lily. They seem a bit reluctant, but they call her down.

She's all cowed and quiet, and when Dr. Barnardo asks if she's happy, she starts to say she's very grateful and then bursts into tears. Barnardo realizes something bad is going on, but then his assistant comes in and tells him he's going to be late for some big fundraising do, and so he just tells Lily to be a good girl and leaves.

I don't understand anything about this. I don't understand why she doesn't tell him the truth straight out—that's what he's come for, after all, to make sure she's okay. It's her one chance to get sent somewhere else. And I don't understand why he tells her to "keep her honor" instead of promising to come back or do something.

I know I'm supposed to forget about my voice, but I also don't understand how I'm supposed to be quiet and subdued while making sure the people in the back row can hear me. And I can't imagine how I'm going to be able to cry when I actually feel super mad at every character in the scene.

So. There we are, with Erin and Ron, who play my foster parents and whom I've barely met, walking through the scene, and I can tell I'm terrible. We're mostly going through the mechanics of entrances and exits, where the chairs are and who sits where, what door I come through and when, but even so, I'm so stiff. By the time Stephen thanks us and sends us off, I just want to lock myself away somewhere and cry.

"Hey, how come so glum?"

Kiefer. Just what I need right now.

"Shut up, Kiefer." I break into a trot, heading for the row of portable toilets at the edge of the parking lot. They're gross, but I need privacy, with no questions asked.

* * *

After lunch Will and I have some time off, so we grab a shady spot under a huge maple tree on the farmhouse lawn.

"You okay, Ava?"

He must have noticed I was still a bit upset at lunch.

"Sure." I hesitate. "I'm just having trouble with one scene," I confess.

Will nods, like it's a normal thing. "What's the problem?"

So I tell him—or try to. "I just don't get why Lily doesn't speak up for herself."

Will smiles. "That's because you're a person who never hesitates to speak up for herself."

I fake-punch him in the arm. "I am not—shut up!" Funny how *shut up* can sound so different from one situation to the next. With Kiefer I was serious. Now, with Will, we're just joking around, and I already feel better about that dumb scene.

He lifts his hands in surrender. "Hey, that's a compliment!"

"Oh." I think about it. "You're probably right though. She's so different from me."

A voice floats down from above my head. "A good actor doesn't need to agree with his character to portray him. That's why it's called acting."

It's Kiefer, of course, managing to butt into our conversation, be a sexist know-it-all and insult me all in one sentence. I am starting to really dislike him.

"Thanks, Kiefer, that's super helpful." I aim my best death glare at him, but he just shrugs and saunters off.

*   *   *

"Let's talk about Lily." After a second run-through of the scene with the reverend and his wife, Stephen has asked me to bring my lunch into his office. Am I about to be cut from the team?

"I know I suck at that scene," I blurt out. *Very professional, Ava. Why don't you just invite him to fire you?*

"It's a very challenging scene," says Stephen. "You don't have much time, or many words, to convey what's going on with Lily. I thought it might help if we talked about what life might have been like for Lily, why she acts the way she does."

"Okay." My stomach relaxes, and only then do I realize how knotted up it was. I guess I'm not getting fired, at least. I take a bite of my sandwich to give myself thinking time.

"I guess..." I suck at my lemonade straw. "I guess I don't understand why she's the way she is in this scene. I mean, I know that they beat her, or at least Mrs. Talmadge has. We learn that when she writes a letter to Walter. But why does that make her so...I dunno, so timid? She was spunky before. Brave. And why doesn't she tell

Dr. Barnardo what's happening? Isn't that what he's there for—to see if she's all right?"

Stephen nods. His wrap has a lot of red sauce oozing out of it, and he swallows and carefully dabs at his beard with a napkin before speaking. "It's hard to imagine how completely alone these kids were, once they were sent to a family. They literally had nobody. They wrote letters to their siblings, not knowing where they were, and never got a reply because the letters were never delivered. There was no phone, no help line, no Children's Aid. They were farther from home than they could imagine, in a completely strange country—so if they ran away, where could they go? They were completely dependent on the families who took them in."

He looks at me. "Think about what that would feel like. Let's make it personal. Imagine your parents die in a car accident, and the officials who are supposed to look after you send you to work, say, for some complete strangers on a ranch in Australia. They speak English, but not your English. They treat you like an unpaid farmhand and beat you, or maybe don't feed you, if they aren't satisfied with your work. You have no cell phone, no TV, no radio, nothing. No contact with your past life. There are no buses, and anyway, you have no money for one. There's just miles of dry land in every direction, and sheep, and a truck you don't have the keys for. What options do you have?"

Whoa. I'm tempted to crack a joke about it, but I don't. I make myself really think about being completely at somebody's mercy like that. It's an awful thought.

Stephen's watching me. He nods at whatever he sees on my face. "Some kids were lucky. They were raised by warm-hearted people who cared about them and gave them a good life. Some weren't so lucky. And some really never got over the fear and loneliness."

I'm starting to get it now. But...

"I still don't understand why she doesn't tell Dr. Barnardo how things are when he asks her point-blank."

"Mmm-hmm." Stephen considers his next words while I chew. "You know, even today a lot of children who are abused never say anything about it. There are a lot of complicated reasons for that, but one pretty clear reason is they are afraid of the consequences. So let's consider. If Lily tells her troubles to Dr. Barnardo, what might happen?"

"Well, I guess the first thing is, Mrs. Talmadge would likely get all huffy and deny it."

"Right," says Stephen. "And remember, back then it was considered completely normal, a parent's right, to whip a wayward child. So you have the word of a very upright, respected member of the community, saying either that it didn't happen or that Lily misbehaved badly enough to deserve it, against the word of a sly little London street urchin. Who do you think they will believe?" He holds up a hand against the protest he sees on my face. "I know, Lily's not like that. But plenty of people in the community would look down on these kids and see them as untrustworthy."

I think about that. Stephen continues, "Here's the other thing. If Dr. Barnardo *doesn't* come through and take her away from there, what will happen to Lily?"

"She'll be punished for speaking up. Probably Mrs. Talmadge has already threatened her about it.

Things will be even worse." God, poor Lily. I'm starting to feel horribly trapped just imagining it.

"Good. It's making more sense to you now?"

I nod. And then I stop. "But the reverend."

"Mr. Talmadge?" Stephen looks mildly surprised. "What about him?"

"Well, he's nice."

"Is he?"

"Yeah. At least, he talks about how well Lily is doing."

He just nods.

"So why doesn't he defend her?"

"Against his wife?" Stephen asks.

"Why not?"

He laughs. "First of all, because she would no doubt make him pay with a lifetime of misery."

I smile. "Okay, I can see that."

He grows thoughtful. "But maybe he's not as nice as he seems. Maybe he's just better at hiding it than his wife." He looks out the window, onto the fields. "I think we can do a better job of suggesting that—and maybe help you in the process." He grins, delighted with whatever is in his head, and nods a bunch of times. "Yeah! I like it."

Stephen pushes his chair back and starts clearing away his lunch things.

"So..." I say cautiously. "Um, are we done?"

He looks up, as if surprised I'm still there. "Oh, yeah." He checks his phone. "And I'm due somewhere else. But thanks for coming—I hope it was helpful. Keep thinking about how someone in Lily's situation, with her feelings, would carry herself and talk. Try out a few things. I think you'll feel different about the scene at our next rehearsal."

I really, really hope he's right.

Seven

We're back at it, and Stephen is making us do a lot of silly warm-ups so we laugh and loosen up. I feel more comfortable with Erin and Ron now. Erin is really goofy and fun, nothing like Mrs. Talmadge. She also seems a bit young for the part, but I guess the makeup department will fix that.

When we get to work, Stephen shifts around the blocking a bit. "I want to suggest a hint of threat from the reverend," he tells us. "So Ron, when Ava comes onstage I want you positioned right by the door to meet her, and then stand quite close behind her as she comes to meet Dr. Barnardo. So you could be acting fatherly or protective, maybe: *Here's my girl!* But it could

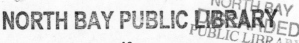

also read as threatening, right? Looming over her."

Ron nods. "Cool."

We try it. I come through the door to meet Dr. Barnardo, and the reverend is right there. I can't help but glance up at him, and he gives me a cold little nod, as if to shoo me ahead.

"Come let me have a close look at you, girl," says Gary, who plays Barnardo.

I take a step forward, and Ron unexpectedly lays his arm across my back and grips my shoulder. I flinch involuntarily and try to stifle it.

"YES!" says Stephen. "That's great, yes!"

Ron says his next line. "Like I said, Doctor, the girl is very obedient and willing to do whatever is asked of her." He tightens his grip on me as he says *obedient*, and, I swear I'm not making this up, I get an absolute chill from the feel of it. He's so scary, telling me right through his hand that I'd better be obedient now if I know what's good for me. I wonder suddenly if he's been "asking" me to do more than chores.

It's the creepiest feeling ever, and now it feels completely natural not to meet Dr. Barnardo's eyes, because I'm scared and confused and unsure of the ground I'm on. When he asks me how I'm doing, it's so obvious now that I'm afraid to tell him—but in my heart I'm pleading with him to understand and help me. And when he turns away, it's like someone threw me a life ring but then pulled it back before I could grab it.

Everyone seems pretty excited as we come to the end of the scene. Erin gives a whoop and high-fives me. "Wow, what a leap forward! You made *me* want to cry!"

Stephen's nodding and grinning. "Really nice, people. Ron, that arm gesture—it's perfect. Nice touch. And Ava." I brace myself. I know it was a lot better, but was it good?

"You've found her. That was Lily. We'll have more fine-tuning with this scene, but this is a big breakthrough. Well done." I'm grinning ear to ear—I can't help it. But Stephen's still talking.

"That tiny flinch you gave when Ron touched you—it was just right."

"That's because I wasn't acting," I confessed. "He took me by surprise, and I tried not to jump but failed." They had a good laugh over that, but

Stephen persisted. "So now you have to learn to repeat that involuntary movement. We'll get there."

I can't wait to find Will. Being Lily in that scene feels horrible, yet getting her right makes me crazy happy.

* * *

Will is supposed to be in the farmyard, working on the ship scene. I'm heading over there when he comes up behind me.

"Hey."

"Will, what're you doing here? I thought you weren't finished for another half hour."

He grins. "On a volunteer mission. Come with me."

He explains as we go. "We're all sitting on these little stools, pretending we're on the deck of the ship, but one has a cracked leg. I volunteered to go get another one because I need the break."

"Where are we going?"

He points. "Storage shed behind the house."

I nod, not that he can see me. Will is a fast walker, and I'm just barely keeping up. "So why did you need a break?" Will doesn't seem the type to run out of energy.

"Swaying and lurching together to suggest we were on a ship came pretty easily to three of us," Will explains. "But there are two kids who are having real trouble doing it in sync. So now we're doing it over and over and over, with clapping and chanting, and, well, since I'm such a good guy, I sacrificed the chance to perfect my sea roll to get little Liam a solid seat."

Before I have a chance to tell him about my breakthrough, we're there.

"I'll just be a second," Will says and heads inside. I hear muffled rummaging and thumping noises. Then Will gives a yelp, and I hear yelling, banging and cursing. He bursts out the door, shouting, "*RUN!*"

I freeze—but then I see the yellow-and-black insects swirling all around him, and I take off. Will is howling and swearing and swiping at his neck and head. I'm terrified they're going to get me too. We dash into the farmhouse and slam the door.

Charlotte looks up, her expression comic-book shock. "What are you—"

"Wasps!" I yell.

Charlotte grabs a newspaper, rolls it up and coolly tracks the one Will has brought in with him. It lands on the window and meets instant death.

"Any more on you?" she asks. Man, she is all business! Will is gingerly feeling his hair, shaking out his shirt. He hasn't stopped swearing and making various kinds of *ow* noises this whole time, although they've come down in volume.

"I don't think so. Do you see any?" he manages between curses. He holds out his arms and turns a slow circle while Charlotte inspects.

The back of Will's neck is swelling up in angry lumps—three at least. There's another on his cheek.

Beth comes in with a bolt of cloth in her arms and quickly abandons it. She's on Will in an instant.

"Will—are you allergic to beestings?"

He shakes his head, cursing again as he feels the swelling on his cheek. "I don't think so. I just hate them! They frigging hurt!"

"But you can breathe all right? Your lips aren't tingly or numb?" She's so serious, I wonder if she's allergic herself.

"Yes. No. Whatever. It just hurts!"

Meanwhile, Charlotte has disappeared into the washroom. She comes back with a wet towel that she drapes around Will's neck.

"Stingers," I blurt out. "Aren't you supposed to get the stingers out?"

Char shakes her head. "That's only for bees. These are yellow jackets. Wasps."

"How do you know?" Will's holding the end of the wet towel against his cheek.

"I killed one, remember?"

Beth has gone to the office and returned with a first aid kit. "Not much in here that will help," she mutters, rummaging through it. "What about calamine lotion?"

"Better than nothing, but not great," says Charlotte. "Is there vinegar in the kitchen?"

"Vinegar!" Beth looks skeptical. "I've heard of baking soda, but—"

"That's bees," says Charlotte, very calm, very definite. "Baking soda for bees. Vinegar for wasps. It's a different kind of venom."

I'm staring at Charlotte. It's like she's turned into some supermedic. "How do you know all this stuff?"

She smirks. "I did a project on biting bugs in sixth grade. Everyone else did raccoons and wolves and bunnies. They thought I was weird—but mine was useful!"

She's busy at the sink, dumping in ice cubes and vinegar and soaking towels in it. One ice-cold, reeking towel goes back around Will's neck. She dabs at his cheek with the vinegar, then gives him a vinegary washcloth wrapped around some ice cubes. "You'll have to just hold this on your cheek." Then her wardrobe persona kicks in. "Beth, do we have something to clip this towel with, to hold it in place?"

A few minutes later, we're heading back. Will dabs at his swollen face with the icy wash-cloth. He looks like a chipmunk with just one cheek stuffed with peanuts.

When we arrive back at the ship rehearsal—without a stool—Kiefer takes one look and bursts out laughing. Of course he does.

Eight

It rains for two days straight. Volunteers come early to mop and sweep the balconies and stairs on the barn and try to keep the "stage" from turning into a mudhole. The July show, which runs in the evening while we rehearse in the day, is rained out both nights.

For rehearsals, we mash ourselves inside, trying to improvise with the backstage lounge and the farmhouse porch. The first day, it feels like a bit of an adventure. The second day is just damp and tiresome, and by the time we're heading home I can't wait to see the sun again.

And we get it, big-time. The next week, it's so muggy and hot that Terry, the stage manager, is bringing buckets of water and towels onto the set so we can wash the sweat off our faces and necks. "Welcome to environmental theater," he says grimly. People come backstage after their sessions, strip off their shirts and douse them in the sink, then put them back on wet. There are fans in the barn, but no air conditioning, of course. We skulk in whatever shade we can find, down bottle after bottle of water, soak our heads—and I still feel completely exhausted at the end of the day.

I'm lucky, in a way. Though we keep practicing everything we've done so far, this week I'm mostly working on my last scene. I'm writing a letter to Walter, telling him about my life with the Talmadges and how much I miss him. It's my biggest scene—and scary in some ways. I'm all alone on the stage, I have a ton of lines, and I have to convey the emotion in them while pretending to write them. The lucky part? I sit down in the shade through the whole thing and hardly have to move.

After one of my run-throughs Mel comes over and nudges me. "See? I told you it would work out."

"What? Oh." I've been so busy worrying about the scene, and surviving the weather, that I've forgotten about my voice. "Is it okay?"

"It's fine. In this heat, everyone gets quieter—too much effort to project." She laughs. "Except your friend Will, of course. That boy is a wonder. Only one I ever met who has to work not to be too loud out here!"

What about me? I want to say. But she's getting there. "You haven't lost any volume at all, which means your voice is already louder. So, no worries, all right?"

* * *

On our first day working in costume, it's a little cooler—thank goodness, because those people wore a lot of clothes! Long sleeves and high necks and heavy stockings. It's even worse for the guys with their jackets and vests layered over everything else. Everyone looks so different, and all of a sudden it feels like we really are in another century. The funny, formal way of talking some of the characters have seems more natural when it matches what they're wearing, and the women move differently in their long skirts and tight collars.

Beth and Charlotte hover around, adjusting here and there and making notes, and we start organizing our costume changes. I've never had to do a costume change in a play before—I have one raggy outfit for my first scene, then a kind of uniform dress in the Barnardo home, and then I layer an apron overtop of that for the scenes at the Talmadges'. Some of the actors are playing multiple characters and will be madly stripping down and redressing all through the show. So there's a lot to figure out about where exactly each outfit will be, who will need help to be ready on time and whether any of the costumes need to be altered so they are easier to get in and out of.

In the afternoon we do our first tech run, nailing scene changes into place and figuring out everyone's entrances and exits. The stage manager makes notes about prop placement and who does what where.

Two hours in, Will groans into my ear. "This is *sooo* boring!" He's right. It really is.

We're in the first row of bleachers, where we can be out of the way but ready for our scenes. The whole cast is either in the seats or standing around on the periphery of the stage. Ron is doing a crossword puzzle. Lots of people are bent over their phones.

Will gets called in for a scene he does with some of the younger kids. They've been fidgety and whiny, despite the child-minder's efforts to keep them happy. Now they are practicing a scene where they have to lie hidden out in the field for quite a while. Then, on cue, they start singing a hymn, get up and walk down the path through the high grass and onto the stage. They do it a few times, only to be stopped, sent back to a spot closer or farther away and then asked to do it again. I'm not part of that scene, so I can see what a cool effect it is, having first the music and then these kids appear out of nowhere, but both the waiting around and the fussy repetitions are getting to me too.

Kiefer flops into the chair beside us.

"What a waste of time," he mutters. "Sitting around all day instead of practicing."

I do a mental eye roll.

Kendra leans over from the row behind us. "Better not let the stagehands hear you saying that. You might find yourself stuck in the dress, with your regular costume mysteriously lost."

I snigger, imagining it, and then reality hits. We have only one more week of rehearsals, and then we open. Will we be ready? Will *I* be ready?

Nine

"C'mon, Mom, it's a *cast party*! Of course I'm supposed to be there!"

My family is back from their camping trip, and I'm (mostly) glad to be home too. Char's mom is really nice, and it was fine staying there for a while, but I feel more myself at home, you know? For one thing, Char and her mom are both really quiet, orderly people, and their apartment is...well, very quiet and orderly. Compared to them, I am this big, loud, messy, sprawling person. I really tried not to strew my stuff all over Charlotte's room, but it was hard, especially with our scramble to get ready and out the door every morning. Now I can leave my clothes lying around on the floor where they belong (haha) and help myself from the fridge whenever I want. It's even kind of nice to be joking around and fighting with my bratty brother, Brandon.

But the parental oversight? Ugh.

The July play, *Dancehall Darlings,* is closing Saturday, and there's a cast party afterward. The play is sold out, but we can watch it sitting on the grass beside the bleachers. Everyone over the age of twelve is invited to the party. *Of course* I really want to go, and I want to stay until the last shuttle at midnight. But I'm normally supposed to be home by ten. I try again to explain.

"The party is after the play, so it won't even *start* till around ten. And we have the day off tomorrow, so I can sleep in!" All that's happening on Sunday is some setup for our play. Then we rehearse solidly, in costume, Monday through Wednesday. Dress rehearsal's Thursday morning, with a preview performance Thursday night.

Mom frowns. "It's an adult party, Ava. There's going to be drinking."

I fight back an eye roll. "Trust me. Stephen and Amanda will *not* be giving the kids booze." I am sure this is true. They treat us like adults when it comes to acting, but they also keep a close eye on us. I'm not so sure about the other adult cast members, but I keep that to myself.

And then...sweet victory. "Okay, we'll meet you at the shuttle drop-off then." Before I can go all giddy on her, Mom sighs and pins me with her most serious face. "*But.* You will call me at ten thirty, and you will answer all my questions, and if I want to talk to Stephen at that point, you will find him so I can."

I'm nodding. *Okayokayokay.*

"I mean it, Ava. Set a reminder on your phone, because if you don't call, we are getting in the car and coming down there to bring you home. I'm not thrilled to be staying up past midnight, so it won't take much to change my mind."

* * *

Dancehall Darlings is a musical. It's clever and fun to watch, the lead actors are crazy good, and the audience loves it—there's lots of laughter and a standing ovation at the end. I can't help wondering if our slower, more serious play will get as good a response.

The audience shuffles out, and the set is replaced by tables loaded with food. The actors reappear in their own clothes, and after everyone gets a plate of food and a drink, Stephen stands up and gives a speech thanking everyone. Then the party starts.

The barnyard is crammed with people eating, talking and laughing. Kiefer has marched over and plopped himself down in the midst of the *Dancehall* leads. They are mostly from Toronto and all have impressive theater bios. I marvel at his nerve—and kind of admire it. I stick pretty close to my friends and the other kids.

Besides Will and Kendra and Char, there's a small army of volunteers I'm just getting to know—Tiegan and Josh, who are stagehands, Melissa, who works at the concession stand, Finn, who helps with makeup and hair, and a few more. It's fun to be hanging out all together for once.

There's a fire pit behind the farmhouse, and before long some of the guys are dragging coolers over there and lighting the fire. We're just heading over when Charlotte tugs at my elbow.

"I'm heading back now."

"What?" I stare at her. "Why?" It's barely ten o'clock.

"My mom and I head out to that cottage tomorrow morning. I have to pack. So I'll see you in a week." Charlotte's mom has insisted that their family vacation time requires Charlotte's presence. In fairness, I guess it's not a "family" vacation if only one person goes.

"Yeah, see ya." The costumes are all made, and the assistant from *Dancehall* is helping Beth with costume changes and adjustments, so there won't be any problem with Charlotte being away. Still, it will be strange to be here without her.

* * *

At the campfire, I feel less like a little kid who snuck into an adult event and more like I belong. Guitars come out, and a mandolin—there are a lot of good musicians in the *Dancehall* cast, and we have some of our own. There are a lot of songs I don't know, but a few that I do. Will seems to know tons of songs and bellows them out with his usual enthusiasm. It's a good thing he can actually carry a tune. I'm not at all self-conscious about joining in, because I'm sitting beside Will and he's totally drowning me out.

Between songs there are lots of stories of funny things that happened during the run. Will gets a star turn recounting the wasp attack. He manages to turn it into a hilarious slapstick comedy, with him climbing up on some old bucket to reach the top stool and then tumbling down, with the chair clutched as a shield, when the wasps started pouring out. He ends the story with Kiefer's demanding, *So why didn't you get the stool?!*

I get laughing so hard I'm suddenly in danger of peeing my pants. Three cans of pop and a laugh attack add up to trouble.

"I'm going for a pee," I say to Kendra as I get up.

"Do you want a flashlight?" She's rummaging in her purse.

"No, I'm fine. I know the way." There are solar lights along the path to the house, and a couple of spotlights out front. It's not until I round the corner, where the row of portable toilets is screened by a tall lilac hedge, that the dark descends.

I grope my way to the first door and step up into it. The door bangs shut behind me, sealing me in a pitch-black, evil-smelling cell. *Ugh*—the toilets are at their worst at the end of the night, after pretty much the entire audience has used them. I have to feel my way to the seat, praying no one has peed on it. I do my business quickly, trying not to breathe and keeping the door open a crack with my foot. Then I burst out into the fresh air.

There's a little step from the floor to the ground, and I just have time to remember this as I half fall out the door. My arms pinwheel as I lurch across the grass, trying to regain my balance. Then my toe catches on something, and I pitch headlong through the air. My hands fly up by themselves to catch me before I land on the gravel path. As my left hand hits, it twists into one of the little gullies the rain has carved into the path. Searing pain shoots up my arm, from the heel of my hand to my elbow. I roll heavily onto my back, cradling my arm. Tears are running down my face, and it's like I'm only just hearing the shriek I made when I hit the ground.

"Ohgod, ohgod, ohgod..." I'm afraid I'm really hurt, and I'm alone in the dark, and the pain is so bad it's making me want to throw up. I try to sit up, but just letting go of my hurt arm sends a wave of pain right into my guts, and I do retch.

"Ava?" I see a flashlight beam waving in the darkness, and then I hear Will's voice again.

"Ava! Are you okay?" He rushes up to me. I'm crying, and I want to choke back my tears and put on my big-girl face, but I can't. "Geez, what happened?"

"I hurt my arm...Will, it really hurts. Can you help me sit up?"

He takes hold of my good arm under the elbow—because I can't make myself let go of my wrist—gets another arm around my ribs and somehow gets me upright. He peers at me. "Amanda was worried that you didn't have a flashlight and sent me after you. Did you trip in the dark?"

I shake my head. "I fell out of the toilet." I hear how that sounds and start giggling despite myself, and Will laughs too, but then I get jostled, and a new wave of pain puts an end to that.

"Are you okay for a few more minutes?" Will asks. "I'll go get Stephen—that looks like it might be serious." He puts the flashlight in my lap—"So nobody runs over you, haha"—and disappears into the dark.

I sit there in the grass, which is turning wet, in the night, which is turning cool, shivering and trying not to think the only thought in my head.

What if my arm is broken?

Ten

Stephen brings his car around, and Will helps him load me into the car. He surprises me by jumping in the back seat.

"It's okay, Will, you can go back to the party," says Stephen.

"No way. I'm going. Ava should have a friend with her." I feel this gush of gratitude—I wouldn't have asked him, but I am so glad to have him with me.

"Thanks, Will." My voice sounds weird—small and scared. It makes me *feel* more scared to hear it. I clamp my lips together.

"Do you have a phone with you?" asks Stephen. "You can call Ava's parents while I drive. Let her know we're taking her to Emerg." He flashes me a smile. "Hopefully, it's just a sprain.

They can hurt like the devil, but get a proper bandage on it and it feels a lot better. A young sprout like you will heal up in no time." I know he must be thinking furiously about what to do if I can't be in the play—no, I'm *not* going to think about that! I stare straight ahead, cradling my arm and concentrating on not crying.

Will snakes his hand over my backrest and squeezes my shoulder. "Almost there." I nod. His hand is warm on my bare shoulder, and I realize I'm chilled and shivering.

I guess he notices too. He pulls his hand away and I want to grab it back, but of course I can't. I hear his seat belt unclip and squirmy movements, and then he's leaning forward and carefully draping his plaid shirt over me. And the pleasantly distracting thought comes to me. *Will really is a sweet guy.*

* * *

It's one thirty in the morning, and I am finally going home—in a cast. My arm feels tight and hot under the plaster, and my wrist throbs steadily. I'm exhausted, but there is no way I'll be able to sleep.

My whole summer has been ruined, and there's no understudy for Lily, so someone will have to stand in for me, reading from the script, and it will suck, and it's my fault.

Mom arrived at the hospital about thirty seconds after we did and shooed Stephen and Will away. I was glad, because by then I really needed to cry and didn't want to be a baby in front of them. Now she bundles me into bed with a cushion under my arm and gives me one of the pain pills the doctor prescribed. "What you need now is sleep," she says firmly. "In the morning we can take stock."

The doctor who set my arm couldn't understand why I was so upset. "It's just a greenstick fracture," she said, trying to reassure me. "Not even broken all the way through. You'll heal up beautifully. A few weeks in a cast, and you'll be right as rain." *A few weeks.* It might just as well be a few years.

I lie in bed, staring up at the ceiling, listening to the throb of my wrist. It just says one thing, over and over.

Stupid, stupid, stupid, stupid.

* * *

I wake up with a start in the morning. First I feel the unfamiliar drag of the cast as I try to turn over. Then all the sore places in my body wake up and yell at me. I groan and take stock. The palms of my hands are scraped and stinging, my shoulder aches, a spot on my hip feels rubbed raw. My broken arm, though, feels surprisingly good. I lift it experimentally and it gives a little throb of protest, but nothing like last night.

It's not much consolation. Better or not, I'm still out of the play.

"Breakfast or lunch?" Mom asks when I finally get up and show myself in the kitchen. I'm surprised to see it's almost noon—it didn't seem like I slept much at all.

"Breakfast." I'm starving, but I also have a jumpy, upset stomach. Breakfast food will go down easier.

Mom gives me another painkiller with my juice, and I spend most of the afternoon sleeping or just sitting around, feeling sorry for myself and guilty for screwing up the play. The phone rings at about three, and I hear my dad say, "Oh hi, Stephen...yes, a minor break."

He snakes his head around the door, gestures at the phone and raises his eyebrows in a question. I shake my head frantically. *NO!* I can't face talking to Stephen right now.

"Asleep now, I'm afraid, but she's doing fine… yes, yes, I'll tell her. Of course…and thanks for calling."

Dad comes into the family room, where I'm staring at but not actually reading Brandon's comics. "Stephen wants to talk to you when you're able. He said he'll call this evening."

I nod miserably.

Dinner brings more fun. Brandon has been at a friend's all day. Now he can hardly eat his dinner for laughing at the fact that I hurt myself coming out of a toilet. "Can I sign your cast?" he begs. "I'll draw a toilet bowl with my name shooting out of it!" He chews, kind of, swallows and launches in again. "No, better, I'll draw teeth around the toilet seat, like the sarlaac in the Great Pit of Carkoon!"

"Haha." It's hard to eat with just one hand, and I hate needing to have my food cut up for me. Dad says I'll be able to use my left hand a bit once the swelling goes down, but right now I basically have a big heavy club hanging off my elbow, so it's hard to picture.

Mom intervenes—finally. "That's enough, Brandon. If you're done your dinner, clear your plate and go hang out your swimsuit and towel on the line. You just dumped them on the deck."

A phone rings—mine this time, from inside my purse. "It's likely Stephen," Dad says. "I gave him your number. You need to talk to him this time, Ava."

I get to the phone just in time and am heading to my room as I answer. *Don't cry*, I order myself. *Just. Don't. Cry.*

Eleven

Monday morning, four days until opening night. I'm at the farm, but I wish I wasn't. It just makes me feel worse to be here. But Stephen asked me to come in for a meeting if I felt well enough. I guess he wants to organize passing my part on to someone else.

We're on the couch in the backstage lounge, not in his office, but it's just us so far. He asks how I'm doing, if I'm in much pain.

"Not too bad." By dinnertime last night my wrist was throbbing again, and I had to take a couple of painkillers and prop my arm up against my chest while I watched TV, but it's not hurting now.

"Did the doctor give you any restrictions on what you can do?"

Weird question. "Not really. Just not to get the cast wet."

There's something I have to say, and it might as well be now.

"I'm sorry. I messed up everything." And now, *crap*, my eyes are stinging and my throat has gone all tight. I promised myself I wouldn't do this!

"That's life," says Stephen. "Stuff happens. I'm just glad you're not too badly hurt." He clears his throat and gets down to business. "So I wanted to talk to you about what we'll do with your part."

I nod miserably. "Will you ask Kendra to take it over and double up her roles?" We never appear onstage together, so it would be possible, I guess.

He frowns. "Maybe. But I spoke with Amanda about it yesterday, and we think, if you're game, we can still make it work with your cast."

You're insane. That's what I want to say. It's ridiculous! I have a fleeting, horrible vision of me onstage as Lily, and nobody even paying attention to the character because they're all staring at the cast.

I'm tongue-tied for once, but I must be shaking my head because Stephen hurries on.

"Just hear me out. We'll reblock the scenes so you don't have to use that hand—you're right-handed, yes? So it shouldn't be too hard. Bring the sleeves down on your dress, maybe see if Beth can work up a flesh-colored cover so the cast is not so eye-catching."

Oh no. This really seems to be what Stephen wants, but I just don't see how it can work.

"It won't fool anybody," I protest. "Look at this thing—it's like a big, heavy log hanging off my arm."

"And that's the part that will be down to you," says Stephen. "There's a way people in a cast move, especially early on, when they're not used to it. You'll have to learn to hold yourself differently, as if your arm is just as light and natural feeling as before. It's a challenge, and there's not much time, but—"

"Are you kidding me?"

I jump at the sound of Kiefer's voice. Where did he come from? I crane my neck and see him standing against the counter, openly eavesdropping.

"There's no *way* she can do that!" he says. I can't believe him, barging in like this—as if anyone cares what he thinks about it.

Stephen shoots him a look that clearly says, *You are interrupting*, but Kiefer is so wound up he doesn't notice. "It's a terrible idea. That big cast will be a horrible distraction for everyone. It will make us *all* look stupid!"

And then I get mad. I don't know if I'm madder at his assumption that I'm not good enough to pull it off or the fact that all he really cares about is how *he'll* look.

And recklessly, for no better reason than to spite Kiefer, I turn back to Stephen and say loudly, "I'll do it! If you really think it's possible, I'll do it."

His wide grin tells me he really was hoping I'd say yes. Kiefer is silent. Stephen turns to him and says, "Thanks, Kiefer, for your help with this meeting. Now, since we open in just a few days, perhaps you could get back to whatever it is you are supposed to be doing and leave the directing to Amanda and me?"

Kiefer's sunburned face flushes even redder. He glowers at me on the way out. I give it right back to him.

"Right, we have work to do." Stephen pops up from the couch, then stops himself. "Uh...did one of your parents drive you here?"

My mom has taken the morning off work. "Yes, she's waiting for me in the parking lot."

"Let's go talk with her."

Ten minutes later I'm back at the farm for real, with a bottle of painkillers in my pocket and a promise to phone my mom at work if I crash and need to come home early.

"We'll look after her," Stephen promises.

"Sorry about the interruption back there," he says to me. "I should have met with you in my office, I guess."

"Why didn't you?" I had been wondering.

"I wanted to be around if Amanda or Terry needed me. But I guess I also thought if you were back in the midst of things..."

"I'd be more likely to agree?"

He laughs. "Something like that."

"Well, it kind of worked." I'm trying not to freak out. It felt great to throw it in Kiefer's face, but that doesn't mean he's not right. How can I be ready in only three days?

Twelve

We go to see Beth, who throws herself into my costume adjustments with her usual enthusiasm. She even takes a photo of my cast. Then we're marching back to the barn, Stephen two steps ahead and on his phone with Amanda. "Yeah, she's in. So you'll hand out that revised rehearsal schedule? Thanks. The priority is to get those scenes reblocked...We'll need Terry for that too."

Stephen and Amanda must have been busy yesterday. An entire plan B is ready to go.

We're almost at the barnyard, and I'm suddenly shy. I usually love the limelight, but not now. *Hey, everyone, here's clumsy Ava with her cast!* My feet come to a stop.

"Ava!" It's Will, sitting in the far bleachers. He jumps up and runs over. "Hey, it's great to see you! You're okay?"

I nod. "Yeah. Just embarrassed."

"*Pfft.*" He dismisses that with a wave. "I heard you're still in the play!"

"I bet you did."

Will bursts out laughing, and I do too. I always feel better around Will.

"Okay, so not *everyone* is pleased. But it's great! Seriously, you *are* Lily. This is awesome."

We find a seat in the bleachers. The scene keeps running. Stephen and Amanda and Terry are huddled on the side, and a couple of people come over and whisper, "Welcome back." And it *does* feel great. Maybe I can pull this off after all.

* * *

We start working through the scenes, making a series of little adjustments that put my left arm, whenever it's reasonable, in the background. In my first scene, I'm now sitting at the other end of the table, so my right arm faces out to the audience. Little Treena, who plays my sister, is sitting in my lap and pretty much hides the cast (though it would help if she could stop staring at it). Stephen says, "Ava, don't try to hide your cast. It will just look like you're hiding something. We'll take the spotlight off it with the blocking, but the key here is that you're simply going to *ignore* it. The more you can act like it doesn't exist, the more the audience will forget about it."

It feels impossible. I'm just in a T-shirt (because Beth is working on my costume), so my cast is hanging white and huge off my arm. It's hot and tight and heavy, and I'm still really focused on not bumping it and hurting my wrist.

Terry must see that I'm worried, because he takes me aside just before lunch. "When did you get your cast on?"

"Right after the party."

He nods. "So it's basically brand-new. I broke two bones in my hand last winter, and I know it feels really weird at first."

"Yeah. Like my arm's the size of a tree trunk."

"But you'll be amazed at how quickly you get used to it. Today we'll do the blocking and get everything organized. By tomorrow, you'll already notice a big difference, and what Stephen is saying about ignoring the cast won't seem so crazy."

* * *

Amanda raids the kitchen and concession stand for my lunch. We eat quickly and then reconvene for the scene with the reverend and his wife. Stephen arrives onset, looking pretty excited.

"Don't ask me why I didn't think of this before—just dense, I guess!"

He then announces dramatically, "We don't need to reblock this scene, or the next."

He seems a little disappointed that nobody protests. Finally Terry says, "Okay, I'll bite. Why not?"

Big grin. "Because we're going to *use* the cast. Dr. Barnardo goes to visit Lily, who is being mistreated, and she comes into the scene with an injured arm. Why not? It totally fits!"

He looks at me. "In fact, I think we'll put it in a sling. Yeah...So Ava, don't let anyone sign it or draw on it, okay? Lily wouldn't have had friends with Magic Markers!"

The actors are looking at each other, slowly nodding as they work the scene through in their heads.

"Will we need new dialogue to work it in?" asks Erin.

"I'm not sure," says Stephen. "Maybe just a remark from your character, Erin, when they're talking with Barnardo, about how clumsy Lily is. Let's run the scene and see how it plays out." We take our places, and then he adds, "Hang on. I should call Beth first."

* * *

The scene works perfectly. The reverend's hand on my shoulder is now so full of threat it makes my head spin. I can easily imagine what led up to this moment—Mrs. Talmadge telling the doctor Lily fell down the stairs, the reverend warning Lily to keep quiet.

Gary as Dr. Barnardo lets his eyes play over my arm with an openly worried look. I can feel him wanting to ask about it and chickening out.

As the scene ends, everyone is grinning. Stephen spreads his hands wide and turns to Terry. "Well?"

"It's brilliant." Terry actually sounds a little awestruck. "Hot damn. Brilliant."

Stephen's nodding. "Yeah. Yeah, it's great." Then his face furrows into an exaggerated frown. "There is one problem though."

Erin takes the bait. "C'mon, it was all good! What?"

"If we ever do the play again, we'll have to break some poor kid's arm."

* * *

By the time I get home, my arm is really hurting. I'm dead tired, but my mood is 100 percent better than when I left the house this morning. Brandon can't even find anything to tease me about, because I'm too happy to react.

Mom nags me into an early bedtime, and I'm sure I'll be awake for hours, but almost as soon as I hit the pillow, I sink into silent blackness. The next thing I know my alarm's ringing.

It's Tuesday. Two days to preview.

Thirteen

"**N**ow if this starts hurting, you tell me."
I nod, but Amanda shoots me a hard,
no-nonsense look. "I'm serious, Ava.
If you wreck yourself now, it could screw up
your performance when it counts, so don't be a
hero. I need you to speak up and tell me if what
we're doing is too much."

"Okay, I get it." She has a bunch of blown-up
balloons in her arms, so it's hard to imagine how
I could get injured.

I'm doing my own special warm-ups to get
me used to my cast, and Will has been recruited
to assist.

"Okay, it's just the balloon game. I'll toss
them up, you bat them back and forth and keep

them in the air." She grins at us. "Just a small variation—right hands behind your back."

It's stupidly hard at first—I'm like the slowest, clumsiest balloon batter ever. But it's with Will, so soon we're laughing and out of breath and I'm lunging around clubbing at balloons, breaking the odd one in the process. Amanda just lets us go at it for a while, then calls a halt.

Will high-fives me. "The Mighty Balloon Slayer prevails!"

"Maybe not for long," says Amanda. "Now comes the tricky part. Tea-party balloons."

We raise our eyebrows and she explains. "Now we want to try for some lightness. Delicacy, if you will." She pulls two chairs over and sets them across from each other.

"So. No brutalizing the balloons. Will is going to float them gently your way, and you are going to gently, precisely tap them back."

I snort. "As if."

"You can do it," she says. "Use your fingertips, try to adjust for the weight and speed differences, and see how quick and light you can be."

On the first round, the balloons either go flying past Will's head or land at my feet. It's funny but frustrating. On the second round, my competitive spirit kicks in, and I get serious.

"Whoa. She looks like she wants to kill me!" says Will.

"Not you," I smile. "Just the job." And I land the balloon quite close his feet.

By the end of the third round I've got it. Tap, tap, tap, and the balloons float gently back, more or less, to Will.

We move on to the next exercise.

* * *

The scene with Kiefer that we first worked on in auditions is the hardest to pull off. Every roadblock we run into—the awkwardness of pretending to sew with my hand in a cast, the clunky hug—is made worse, somehow, by Kiefer's eye rolls and sighs. He knows enough not to say anything more, but he shakes my confidence all the same. Then Amanda suddenly snaps her fingers and says, "She needs an embroidery hoop!"

Stephen looks as blank as I feel. What the heck is an embroidery hoop?

"My mother has a couple with her knitting gear," she says. "She said she used them as a teenager, to embroider patches for her jeans. They hold the cloth tight on a little frame, so you can work the stitches. You could easily hold it with your cast hand." Amanda calls her mother, and by lunchtime I have a tight little circle of cloth to hold in my left hand while sewing with my right. It's brilliant.

The hug's a bit harder. "You have to just go for it," says Stephen. "Throw your arms around him like there is no cast. But try not to deck him."

He turns to Kiefer. "And you have to stop flinching! You're hugging your long-lost sister!"

We try again, but it just feels wrong. Kiefer's a fair bit taller than I am, so I have to really raise my arms to go around his neck. It's hard not to knock his head with my clunky arm.

Stephen turns to Amanda. "Should we see if Brad is around?"

"Who's Brad?" I ask.

"Fight coach. He could teach you how to do this safely." He catches my look and shrugs. "Fighting, hugging—there's not so much difference."

Amanda's thumbing her phone, but I have a thought of my own. "Do I have to hug him that way?" I'm not sure Stephen wants my opinion, but he seems to be taking me seriously.

"What do you mean?"

"Well, we've been trying to do this big hug. But maybe instead I could kind of nestle up against him with my arms down around his waist, like he's my protector?"

Amanda gives herself a head smack. "Oh good grief. *Yes.* Of course, yes!"

Stephen's shaking his head. "Sorry, guys, we should have thought of that from the start. I have a habit of doing things the hard way." Then he's right back to business. "Okay, back at it. We're on the clock here!"

Kiefer's tall enough that it works fine. I wrap my arms around his waist and tuck my head in against his shoulder and kind of snuggle in. It feels like hugging a board though—he seems really awkward suddenly.

"Okay, that's good," says Stephen. "Kiefer, you're looking pretty stiff, but that actually works with Walter's character. You'll loosen up as you settle in, but a hint of awkwardness—like he doesn't know how tight he should hold her—is nice."

Kiefer looks upset. "It's just—it's not what we practiced. It throws me off."

"Adapting to last-minute changes is hard," Stephen agrees. "But it's part of the trade." He claps Kiefer on the shoulder. "Don't worry, you're doing great. It will work. Now let's move on."

* * *

In the afternoon Beth appears and asks me to come try on my new costume. She's put looser, longer sleeves on the dress. They have cuffs that won't easily slide back if I raise my arm but are wide enough to fit around the cast. "You can undo the button and roll these back for the second half if they want to show the cast more," she says. "And now—the *pièce de résistance*!"

With a flourish she pulls out what appears to be a limp strip of pantyhose. I want to show some enthusiasm, but I don't really know what I'm looking at.

"Let's see how it fits. Hold out your arm." Soon I have a perfectly fitted "skin" clinging to the cast. The effect is startling—she's matched my skin color really well.

Beth is busy fiddling with the ends. "You have to tuck it in around the edges of the cast here at the hand end. You can do that part yourself—but I am the *only* person allowed to pull this over your cast! I don't want some bozo giving it a bunch of runs."

"It's great, Beth! Thanks!"

She nods matter-of-factly. "I *am* the best." She holds my cast at arm's length and gives it a critical once-over. "Oh, yeah. You'll do!"

*   *   *

Before I know it, it's dress-rehearsal day. Which means we open tonight! My wrist hardly ever hurts now unless I bump it or shake it. Terry was right—the cast feels a lot more like it's part of me. Which is good, because I have more to think about than a stupid cast. This is the biggest, most important play I've ever been in, and I *can't* mess up!

On the shuttle to the farm, I'm suddenly missing Charlotte. I feel jittery and light, like I might float away. I need some of Char's steadiness. I realize with a pang of guilt that I haven't even texted her this week. Then I remember that she's at a cottage on some lake with no cell service—which for some reason her mom thought was a *good* thing.

* * *

Terry starts with our run schedule. "This is your life for the next four weeks," he announces. "Tuesday to Sunday. Shuttle leaves town at quarter to four. You get here at four and eat on-site. Or eat at home and show up by four thirty. Notes and news in the lounge at four thirty-five. Do not miss them! Questions?" He scans the cast and crew assembled in the barnyard. "Then let's put on a show."

Dress rehearsal goes pretty well, I think. There's a bit of fumbling with costume changes backstage, and a prop mishap when Old Walter's mug topples off the table. Treena, who's only four, keeps running her fingers over the new cast covering when she's on my lap.

It's funny, but it's only striking me now how different an open-air play is to stage. For one, you can't black out the stage for scene changes. It all happens out in the open. Now I under-stand why we spent so much time fine-tuning the entrances and exits—they have to be part of the story too.

After we do our last bow, Will finds me backstage. "Ava, you were amazing. You blow me away in that scene with Barnardo."

I let out a long breath. It's just Will, doing what friends do to boost each other, but it still feels really good to hear. "Thanks, Will. They are going to love your Billy—you've made him the best character in the play." It's true. Billy's cheeky humor and good-natured friendship are the bright spot in what is, honestly, a pretty sad play.

Will throws his arm around my shoulders and gives me a squeeze in thanks, and then he leaves it there. I tuck my arm around his waist and lean in a little. It occurs to me that maybe I don't just like Will—maybe I *like* him—and that we'll be at the same school in the fall. That thought brings a little rush of heat to my cheeks.

Then our little moment, or whatever it is, is interrupted—the cast is being summoned.

*   *   *

Stephen's doing the usual pre-show pep talk—*thanks for all your hard work, you've done a tremendous job, yadda yadda yadda*—and I'm not really listening. I'm too full of my own thoughts about the night to come and honestly still amazed that I'm even in the show.

Then he says something that snags my attention.

"Now I want to address something very important before I let you go to rest up for tonight. I overheard someone referring to tonight as 'just the preview.' I appreciate that it was probably said to calm some opening-night jitters, but I want to stress that tonight is *not* a less-important show. In fact, it's the opposite. We offer a Thursday-night preview because it's hard to get reviewers to leave the big city on the weekend and also to give our members the chance for a special viewing. Tonight's audience will include critics from major media, the members whose donations keep this theater alive, and, most important, relatives of the three Barnardo children whose stories are the core of this play. They deserve the very best show we can give them." He pauses for a moment to let that sink in. "So let's go out there tonight and nail it!"

Thanks, Stephen. Now I'm *really* nervous.

Fourteen

'␣ve never been this antsy before a play. I feel
like I might jump out of my own skin.

"Cheer up, ducks—it's all good fun until
someone loses an eye!" Will's Artful Dodger
Cockney accent is so terrible, I have to laugh.
Still, my stomach won't stop flip-flopping.

I'm heading to the toilet for one last pee
("Mind the step!" Will shouts after me) when
Kiefer rushes past me. The door bangs shut, and
then I hear the unmistakable sound of retching.
He comes out wiping his mouth and grimacing.

"God, that's even grosser in a portable toilet."

"Are you sick?" What will we do if Kiefer is
sick? But he shakes his head.

"No, it's just the jitters. I do it pretty much every
opening night. But don't worry." He brandishes

a ziplock bag with a toothbrush and toothpaste in it by way of reassurance.

I'm amazed. Kiefer always seems so confident. But this is not the time for needling each other. "I'm really nervous too," I confide.

He gestures at my cast. "Well, yeah. No wonder."

He really does not make it easy to like him. I escape into the toilet—*mind the step.*

* * *

There is nothing like the feeling of stepping out onto the stage with the stands full of people. I tuck in the ends of my cast cover one last time. *Cast? What cast?* I say to myself, and with one last, deep breath, I think about being Lily, a poor London girl with a big voice and a meek manner. I check that my little brother and sisters are gathered around me, wait for the cue—and off we go.

There are no lights on the stage, so the audience is right there in full view. I see my parents and Brandon in the third row. Thank goodness I told them not to sit right up front. It would be horribly distracting.

I'm also glad my first scene is sitting around the table with the younger kids. With little Treena on my lap and "Annie" and "Jack" beside me, it's easy to focus my attention on them rather than the audience. By the time our dad and Walter arrive on the scene, I'm feeling a lot more settled.

Backstage it's silent, controlled chaos. Actors shuck off clothes and wiggle into different ones, grabbing props on their way back onstage. Stagehands hover, waiting to move wheelbarrows, tables or farm tools. I do my best to stay out of everyone's way.

There's a little glitch when the kids in the field appear. They come on cue, but the singing is ragged, like only a few kids are singing and not in time with each other. But Will soon sets them straight, singing out in his giant voice and pumping his arm in time like a parade master or something. By the time they get close to the stage, they are all singing out properly. A good thing, because one of the adults waiting has to say, "That's the loveliest singing I've heard in many a year."

And the effect is fantastic. In the heat of the afternoon or the muck of a rainy day, you forget what it's like for the audience. In the evening, with the light shafting through the high grass in the meadow and lighting up the far fields, the sky full of clouds and swallows, a distant farmhouse looking not so different than it did a hundred years ago, it's as if those kids magically appear out of another time. It's crazy cool.

I feel like my scene with the doctor goes really well. I actually hear not a gasp, exactly, but some kind of little murmur from the audience when I come out with my cast in full view, supported in a narrow sling looped from my wrist around my neck. But I don't let it distract me—I focus on my lines and on the reverend's tight grip on my shoulder. I think I get it right.

But I guess I relax too much, because I'm going along with my letter in my next scene when I suddenly realize I have skipped a line. I freeze for a second—my heart's pounding and my head feels like it's on fire. So I chew on the end of my pen, like I'm thinking what to write next, while furiously wondering what to do. I realize there's another spot where the line I missed will work fine. I plow on.

As I exit through the barn door, Stephen's waiting on the other side. He bends down to me and whispers, "Nice save."

* * *

And then we're taking our bows. When Will, Kiefer and I go out together, it's just the most amazing feeling I have ever had. Everyone is on their feet and cheering, and my mom is, like, *crying*, and even Brandon is yelling my name.

A four-week run is about three weeks longer than the longest I've ever done. I've been warned that it's hard to keep up your enthusiasm for that long, but right now it's impossible to believe. I feel so giddy and triumphant, I want to burst out laughing and hug everybody—but instead I bow again, smile and head offstage.

When we all go back out together for our final call, I have Treena in my arms. She's pretty freaked by the noise. She ducks her head into my shoulder, and I whisper, "It's okay, Treena. They're clapping because they thought we were good.

You did great!" I joggle her back and forth and get a little smile from her.

"But it's scary," she says.

"You'll get used to it," I say. But that's kind of a fib. I'm sure I'll never get used to this—and I don't want to!

* * *

It feels weird to wake up the next morning to an empty house—my parents are at work, and Brandon is at day camp.

I wander into the kitchen, glance at the table—and suddenly my heart starts to race. Mom has left the local paper, folded to a specific page, with a note: *So proud of you!* It must be a review of the play.

I snatch it up. It's positive, of course—I've often heard my parents comment on how the community paper says nice things about *every* local event—so that doesn't mean much. But then I read:

> *Special mention must be made of the three*
> *talented young performers who play the*

characters of Billy, Walter and Walter's sister, Lily, as children. Will Solomon's high-spirited and energetic Billy is a perfect sidekick to Walter's darker character, and his great comedic instincts bring some welcome laughs to an otherwise somber play. Ava Olejarzyk—

Of *course* they spelled my name wrong.

—gives a moving performance as the unfortunate Lily, who is trapped in an unhappy placement with unkind guardians. Though she has only a few scenes, she punches above her weight in emotional impact. Her finely tuned performance is at its best in a scene with her guardians, perhaps the most disturbing and memorable of the play. And all this with a cast on her arm—that is one spunky young actor!

Okay, I'm flinching at that last part—what a way to ensure everyone who comes to the play after reading this will be watching for my cast!—but

I'm grinning from ear to ear at the rest. So what if it's just the local paper? I'll take it! I read on to see what they say about Kiefer.

> *Kiefer Monroe, already a familiar face in the local Theater Guild, delivers a solid Young Walter. Since Walter, unlike the other two children, has a positive placement experience, it is, perhaps, a weakness of the play that it's not completely clear why Young Walter matures into the angry and seemingly traumatized Old Walter. However, Mr. Monroe does very well with his material. (He is also charmingly awkward in a dress and bonnet!)*

I stare at this last paragraph for a while, trying to puzzle it out. I guess maybe the reasons for Old Walter's anger and shame about being a Barnardo boy are not 100 percent obvious—though being deliberately cut off from his whole family seems reason enough. But why put that *there*, where they're talking about the acting? It looks like they're criticizing Kiefer even though they say they aren't. I picture

Kiefer reading it and feel bad for him. Which is surprising, really, considering how snotty he's been to me.

*　*　*

On the shuttle bus, Will plops down beside me and drops an iPad into my hands. "We made the *Globe*."

The *Globe*? "Is that…?"

"It's big," says Will. "And they liked it." He grins and nudges me. "Specifically, they liked *you*. Read it!" And he points to the paragraph already loaded to the screen.

> *Ava Olejarczyk's affecting performance as Lily is surprisingly mature for such a young actor. It's a pity Lily's story does not feature more prominently in the play…*

Just one line, but it gives me such a boost of confidence. "I guess you're not really supposed to care about reviews. But—" I'm scanning the article, looking for what else it says. Nice stuff about Will and Kiefer too, but—am I imagining it?—is the tone again less enthused about Kiefer? More vaguely positive?

"But damn, it feels good when they like you!" Will finishes my thought. "So why the frown?"

I glance around the bus. Kiefer's mom always drives him to the farm, but I lower my voice anyway. "I'm worried Kiefer's not going to be happy with this. In the local paper too, they said he was good but without anything really specific."

Will nods and does his best to match my quiet tone. "Honestly, I thought Kiefer was a little off last night. I mean, he didn't do anything wrong. But he's normally really good—kind of a jerk, but good—and he wasn't at his best."

I remember Kiefer's bolt for the toilet. "Maybe just opening-night jitters?" I say.

Will nods. "Yeah, maybe. Maybe he's not as confident as he lets on. Hopefully, he'll find his stride again."

Fifteen

iefer doesn't arrive until after we've eaten. At our pre-show meeting he stands by himself at the back and doesn't meet anyone's eye. He is definitely not his usual *look at me* self. I have a bad feeling that tonight's show might be in trouble.

It comes out during warm-ups.

"This is stupid!" Kiefer bursts out in the middle of our stretches. "What is even the point of all this stuff? It's not like we're doing gymnastics out there!" He walks away.

Amanda stares after him, completely stumped. "What...?"

"I'll go," says Will, jumping up. "It won't kill me to miss the vocal warm-ups." He runs after Kiefer.

I kind of want to go too, but I guess we shouldn't gang up on him.

Amanda calls me over. "Do you know what's going on?"

"Not really," I say. "But my guess is he's not happy with the reviews."

Amanda looks dubious. "Really? But the reviews I've seen are really good!"

"Yeah. But Kiefer is...complicated. Maybe they weren't *as* good for him as he expected? But that's just a hunch."

"All right. I'll give Stephen a heads-up. You go get changed, and then maybe check on how they're doing."

I dive into my dress, muss up my hair for the first scene and go in search of the guys.

I find them—with Stephen—on the porch of the farmhouse.

"I suck, that's what the problem is!" Kiefer bursts out. "You should just give the part to someone else. Someone *good!*"

Stephen scratches his beard like he does when he's frustrated. "Kiefer, I picked you for Walter because you *are* good. Your work has been good right from the audition. So where is this coming from?"

"Don't you even read the reviews?" Kiefer looks like he's about to cry. "Ava Olewhatshername is wonderful as Lily. Will Solomon's Billy is a friggin' joy to behold. Kiefer Monroe is all right, I guess."

"Oh good grief." Another furious scratch. "Kiefer, look at me." Stephen's eyes scan the horizon briefly, like he's looking for a place to start.

"First of all, you got good reviews, for crying out loud. Walter is the main character, yes, but Billy and Lily are easier characters to like. Billy is funny and smart-mouthed. Lily is sweet and vulnerable. Walter is a darker, more complex character. So the fact that someone who has seen the play once finds it easier to comment on Lily and Billy has nothing to do with the quality of your performance." Kiefer's shoulders hunch, like he's fending off Stephen's words. Stephen sighs.

"Second. A review is of one night, by one person, with one kind of taste. Every single working actor in this play has had actual bad reviews, and has had to find faith in their own talent and go back onstage. It's part of the gig. You have talent, but that's not enough—you need a thick skin too. So here's your first challenge. To read reviews that are not quite as super good as you'd like, feel the disappointment, and then get back on your horse and prove them wrong. Tonight."

"I don't know if I can." Kiefer's voice is barely audible.

"We'll help you." It's Will, and he motions me over. "Won't we, Ava?"

I don't know how, but I know we have to try. "Yeah, of course. Kiefer, I've known since the audition we did together that you're a better actor than I am. I've learned a lot working with you." *Yeah, like how to work with people I dislike.* "I know you can get your mojo back."

Stephen looks at us. "Okay, then. I think maybe your friends will do a better job of convincing you than I can, so I'll leave you to it. Just keep an eye on the time. I don't want you running on set half dressed! And call if you need me."

He leaves us alone. None of us know what to say. Then Will ventures, "So, buddy. Stephen has spoken. We all think you're a great Walter, and we need you tonight. What can we do to help?"

Kiefer glances at each of us. "Why would you even want to bother?"

Will launches into his bad Cockney. "Number one, if we ain't got no Young Walter tonight, we're all scuppered, Squire!" Then he drops the act, his face serious. "And number two, come on, man! We're all in this together. We don't want to see you hurting over this thing. It should be fun."

"Fun. It's fun for you?" Kiefer asks.

"Well, yeah," says Will, like it's obvious.

"You, Ava?" Kiefer turns to me.

I nod. "I mean, it's hard work, and scary a lot of the time. But I really like it too."

He thinks a while, then blurts out, "Let me ask you something. Did you think I was as good as usual last night? Because I felt, all night, like it wasn't going that well."

Will and I exchange glances, not sure of what to say. But he asked, so I answer honestly.

"I guess...I felt like you were a little, um..." I'm not sure what the right word is. "Restrained? Compared to during rehearsal, I mean."

"What about you?" He trains his eyes on Will.

"Yeah, I guess. Like maybe you just needed to loosen up a little, have more fun with it."

"*Fun* again." He shakes his head.

I have an idea. "Kiefer, I think maybe Will keeps using the word *fun* because his character *is* fun—fun to play, fun to watch. You and I, we don't really have fun characters. But..." I'm reaching here. "Maybe you were playing it a little safe?" *What does that even mean?* "Maybe," I offer slowly, "maybe because it was opening night, and Stephen put all that extra pressure on us to be awesome, it was harder to get into *being* Walter." I am remembering that scene I had so much trouble with until I was able to really feel what Lily would have felt. "Does that make any sense?"

Kiefer nods just slightly, like he's thinking it over. "Yeah...maybe. Maybe I was trying too hard not to screw up, instead of..."

Will catches my eye and taps his wrist—there's no watch there, but I get the meaning.

"Kiefer, it's time to go get ready."

His head jerks up. "Oh god. How am I gonna—"

"We're with you, man." It's Will, and his voice is firm and confident. "We'll do it together. Billy and Walter—we're best buddies, remember?"

Kiefer barks out a strangled laugh. "Okay. Let's go then."

* * *

The audience is lining up outside the box-office gate when we rush into the barn. Terry looks like he's ready to kill us. "Where were you?" he hisses. "Get your little late butts ready, *now!*"

"Sorry, guys," Kiefer whispers as we hurriedly smudge our faces with London street dirt. "And, you know, thanks."

Mind. Blown.

I'm nervous about Walter's first scene, when he comes in with our dad from chimney sweeping. But he arrives on cue, and since he doesn't have to say or do much in that scene, it's a good warm-up. And once Kiefer makes that first entrance, he's fine.

More than fine. For the first time, our brother-sister scenes feel like more than acting, like there really is a bond between us.

And Kiefer gets better as he goes along. He's a little stiff at first, but by the time he hits the scene in the dress, he's playing up the awkwardness and getting some laughs, but then hugging me fiercely, like he really means it, when we say goodbye. In the scene on the ship, where he calms the kids down by singing, he sings out like an angel.

At intermission he's smiling, and I realize how rarely I've seen him actually look happy. Is that partly our fault for shutting him out? He wasn't easy to include, but there has definitely been a "me and Will versus Kiefer" thing going on, I can't deny it. When he comes over to hang out with us, he looks kind of shy, like he's not sure he'll be welcome. But Will slings an arm around his shoulder and says, "You *are* Walter tonight, buddy! And admit it—it is fun!"

And Kiefer actually laughs and says, "Well, more fun than last night, anyway."

* * *

On Sunday when I go to put on my costume, Charlotte is there, holding out my dress.

"You're home! You didn't call!" I fling my arms around her and actually do conk her on the shoulder.

"Ow. Yes, just this aft. I wanted to surprise you."

She holds up my cast. "So, seriously—you went and broke your arm without me?"

We both laugh. "Sorry about that. Are you working or in the audience?"

"Tonight I'm in the audience, with my mom. Beth just let me come backstage. But I'll be back here next week."

"Come after the show and hang with us," I urge. "You could take the shuttle back."

She nods. "I'll try to talk Mom into it."

There's no more time to talk.

"I gotta get back—I left Mom in line so we can get a good seat." Another hug. "I can't wait to see the whole play put together, and you bumbling around with *that*."

"With what?" I ask, holding my arm out obediently as Beth appears with my cast cover. "I do not have a cast, or a broken arm, or anything out of the ordinary at all."

"If you say so. Okay, then, see you after!"

* * *

The run, as we were warned, goes on and on. We have another heat wave, with stacks of towels backstage for mopping away sweat, and the audience a sea of fanning programs. We have a rain-out. And there's a cold making the rounds. Luckily, no one gets too sick to perform.

We put on a good show, and we have a good team. I can't say Kiefer has suddenly become nice. But he makes an effort, and so do we. When we hold hands to take our bows every night, it feels good, like, *Yeah! We did it again!*

Honestly, it's a relief to hit our last performance. And yet I can hardly keep from bawling on our last bow. I actually do cry when my dad comes to pick us up after the cast party.

Sixteen

One week of vacation left, and then school. My grandma has come to stay so that my brother and I can have "unstructured time" (my mom's words) and "laze around" (my dad's). And that's pretty much all I do—laze around. A couple of times I go over to Char's and hang out at her building's pool, but I don't really feel like doing much. I spend a lot of time on the couch watching Netflix.

Grandma must have said something to Mom, because on Wednesday after dinner she takes me aside.

"So...are you having a little trouble coming back to everyday life after your summer on the farm?"

I shrug. "I don't know...I guess so. Everything just seems...I don't know, boring."

She nods. I'm surprised at how sympathetic she seems—I expected a "snap out of it" lecture. "I worked at a summer camp for three years, and every year when I came home, I moped around for a week. It drove my parents insane."

Ha. It's funny to think of her acting like me. "What got you out of it?" I asked.

"School, I guess," she answers. "Something new to do."

School. I should be excited or at least nervous about school. I'm starting high school, after all. But I'm neither.

"What do you say to a little shopping therapy?" says my mom. "You need some school clothes, right?"

I really do. "Can we take Char?" It will be more fun with Charlotte. Also, even though she doesn't fuss much with her own clothes, she always knows exactly what's in style and what looks good on me.

"Sure," my mom says, then pulls out her phone to check the time. "A bit late to start now though. Let's plan to go right after dinner tomorrow." She smiles. "Ask Charlotte to come for dinner—it'll save time."

* * *

On Friday I get my cast off. The wait at the hospital feels like hours. When the nurse finishes cutting through the plaster, I can see that my arm is all white and shriveled and—*ew*—the skin's flaking off it.

I must look horrified because the nurse pats my arm and says, "Don't worry. With a little air and use, it will start to look normal soon." Great. I'll be starting high school looking like I have leprosy or something. I'd rather have the cast.

* * *

The last long weekend of the summer goes by pretty quickly, thanks to my parents insisting that we all go camping at a nearby provincial park. On Monday night it finally hits me—*I start high school tomorrow!* How will I even get up so early? I've been sleeping late for a month now. What if I miss the bus? How will I find my homeroom? What if there's no one I know in my classes? My mind goes round and round in circles.

When the alarm goes off at seven, I feel horribly tired and groggy.

I blast the shower right on my face to make myself wake up. It *is* nice to have a regular shower again, no messing around with a plastic bag over my arm. Then into a new top and old jeans (don't want to look too eager).

I don't feel hungry, but my mom won't let me out the door unless I eat something. I appease her with a bowl of cereal with a banana sliced over it, then throw my lunch into my backpack, and I'm off.

Char is on my bus, and it's nice to be able to walk into the school together. We have different homerooms, though, so we soon part ways.

The morning feels long—Math, English, Geography. Char's in my Geography class, so we don't have to worry about finding each other at lunch.

We line up at the cafeteria to buy drinks and scope out any familiar faces. I spot Sadie and Carla from my old school, and we all grab a table together. In a few minutes Emily appears, and we wave her over. Safety in numbers, right? They all seem way more impressed with high school than I am—gossiping about cute boys in their classes and people's clothes and who they've seen. So far, for me, it's just school, only bigger.

I'm heading back to my locker after lunch when a familiar voice booms down the hall. "AVA! Hey, there you are! Wait up."

Will bounces like he has springs on his sneakers. "How's it going? What classes do you have?" He notices my arm. "You got your cast off! That's awesome."

Geez, he's contagious. I'm suddenly happier than I've felt all day—especially after we compare schedules.

"You're taking Drama, I hope?" Will asks.

"Yeah, of course."

"Cool! So there's one class we have together." It turns out we also have our last class together—Information and Communications Technology, whatever that is.

"Did you see the notice on the bulletin board?" Will seems quite excited—much too excited for a school notice.

"Um, what bulletin board?"

He checks the time. "We're good. Okay, c'mon!" He actually takes my arm and starts pulling me down the hall.

Beside the office there's a large bulletin board. On it is a big, brightly colored poster. Will flings out his arm at it. "Ta-da!"

I start to read, and I can actually feel my pulse speeding up.

AUDITIONS NEXT WEEK!

Preliminary auditions for the fall musical, **Back to the Eighties***, will take place in the small gymnasium on Wednesday and Thursday, Sept 13/14. Be there at 3:45, prepared to sing a short musical piece and read a scene.*

Students interested in production roles (costumes, sets, stagehands) should also come to the small gym on Friday at 3:45.

Audition times for lead parts will be announced next week.

Contact Ms. Gooderham, Room 322, for more information.

"So you're going, right?" Will demands.

I want to. But..."I'm not that much of a singer."

He waves it away. "I heard you sing. You're fine. And they'll probably only give ninth-grade kids chorus roles anyway. But it's getting on the radar, right? They always do a drama in the spring—no singing required."

I feel the grin spreading across my face, wider and wider. "I'm in. Which day do you want to go?"

"The first day, obviously! And if you want to practice your song in front of an audience in the meantime, I'm your man."

I'm already thinking about what I should sing. And wondering what the play is about. And whether I should have a résumé. No, I decide. Not yet, anyway.

That thought leads me to Kiefer and his "babe in arms" theater credit. I'm tempted to tell Will about it—but then I let it go. Now that I know Kiefer doesn't always feel as high and mighty as he acts, a laugh at his expense just seems mean. Instead I ask, "Hey, Will, do you know where

Kiefer is this year?" I know Kendra's at the French Immersion high school across town, but Kiefer never mentioned his "real life"—not to me, anyway.

"Yeah, his parents are sending him to some fancy private school in Toronto. I don't think he's real happy about it either."

So we probably won't be crossing paths any time soon. To my surprise, I'm kind of sorry.

The bell jangles. Time for Drama.

"C'mon then, Ava," says Will. "Don't want to miss our cue!"

I just know it's going to be the best class of the day.

Acknowledgments

I could not have written this book without the help of so many generous people.

First and foremost, thanks go out to Robert Winslow and Ian McLachlan, co-authors of *Doctor Barnardo's Children*, for allowing me to use their play as the production in *Casting Lily*. Robert, who is also founder and creative director of 4th Line Theatre in Millbrook, Ontario, also allowed me to use his beautiful farmyard theater as the inspiration for Mill Pond Farm. Jade O'Keeffe, who played Lily in the first production of the play at 4th Line, shared her memories of that summer with me. While I borrowed both the play and the setting for this book, the characters, the rehearsal process and the play reviews are entirely fictional.

Director Em Glasspool of Mysterious Entity Theatre and the cast of *The Blind Eye*, and directors Drew Mills and Terry Convey of St. James Players and the cast of *Princess Whatshername*, generously allowed me to observe their rehearsals in progress. Karen Hoffman and Keegan Plant gave me a crash course in community theater and production. Finally, Victoria Windrem, with her background in both community theater and YA writing, was the perfect reader to preview and critique this story.

Thank you, all!

HOLLY BENNETT is the author of numerous young adult novels published by Orca Book Publishers, including *Drawn Away*, a modern retelling of *The Little Match Girl*. Holly hasn't been in a play since elementary school, but she knows lots of actors, musicians and "theater people" and loves going to their performances. She lives in Peterborough, Ontario. For more information, visit www.hollybennett.ca.

Titles in the Series

orca limelights